For information address
Disney Press, 1101 Flower Street, Glendale, California 91201.
Printed in the United States of America
First Edition, September 2015
10 9 8 7 6 5 4 3 2
FAC-038091-15243
ISBN: 978-1-4847-2468-2
Library of Congress Control Number: 2014947913
For more Disney Press fun, visit www.disneybooks.com

Disney FROZEN

Olaf's Night Before Christmas

By Jessica Julius

Illustrated by Olga T. Mosqueda

Disney PRESS

Los Angeles • New York

'Twas the night before Christmas and all through the house,
Not a creature was stirring, not even a mouse.

Stockings were hung by the chimney—but why?
Had they gotten too wet? Were they left there to dry?

Elsa was sleeping,
all snug in her bed,
While glittering northern lights
danced overhead.

Anna **snored** softly
while I counted sheep,

Settling myself for a
cozy night's sleep,

When out on the fjord there arose such a clatter,

I sprang from my bed to see what was the matter!

Away to the window I tumbled and rolled.
I pushed out the shutters, and—*brrrrr*—was it cold!
A full moon was out, and it lit up the night
While snow flurries made the world sparkly and white!

★ ⟫⟫⟫⟩ ✳ ❄ ✳ ⟨⟨⟨⟨ ★

Then, grabbing an icicle, what did I spy?
Eight little Svens, flying high in the sky!
The Svens pulled a sleigh. There was someone inside.
Could Sven and his Kristoff be out for a ride?

Straight toward the castle the flying sled came
While the man—was it Kristoff?!—
called out some strange names:

"Now, Dasher! Now, Dancer! Now, Prancer and Vixen!
On, Comet! On, Cupid! On, Donner and Blitzen!
To the top of the turret and over the wall!
Now dash away! Dash away! Dash away, all!"

He sounded so funny. Who was this big guy?

What was a turret, and how could Svens fly?

And then with a ringing,
I heard on the roof
The thumping and bumping
of each little hoof.

Then from behind me,
there came a **strange sound**,
And the whole chimney **shook**
as two feet hit the ground!

FOR SANTA

His boots were all black
and his pants were all red,
But where was the rest of him?
Where was his head!

Then out of the fireplace
the man's face appeared.
He had kind, crinkly eyes
and a fluffy white beard.

Kristoff he wasn't;
this man smelled too nice,
Like snowballs and cookies
and Christmassy spice.

He placed a large bag filled with gifts on the floor.

Was a sale going on at old Oaken's big store?

He brushed off his clothes, then began to unpack,
Pausing for **krumkake** left out as a snack.

This stranger had presents
for Anna and Sven,
For Kristoff, for Elsa,
for all of my friends!

I reached for his coat
and gave two little tugs
And said, "My name is Olaf,
and I like warm hugs!"

He turned with a start, then let out such a giggle
I had to laugh, too, when I saw how he jiggled.

He gave me a hug,
such a wonderful gift.
Then he rose up the chimney,
all lively and swift.

And I heard him call out as he flew out of sight,

"Merry Christmas to all, and to all a good night!"